The Slug, the Snail

and their Tale

With Idioms

Reach for the stars
Ramy! :)

Sara Dutton

Published in 2020 by:

Stellar Books
1 Birchdale
Bowdon
Cheshire
WA14 2PW

W: www.stellarbooks.co.uk
E: info@stellarbooks.co.uk

ISBN: 978-191-0275313

© Sara Dufton 2020

Written, printed and published in the United Kingdom

Illustrations by Freddie Btesh
Cover designed by Sara Dufton

The author asserts her moral rights to be identified as
the author of her work.

All rights reserved.

No part of this publication may be reproduced, stored
in any retrieval system, or transmitted in any form by any
means, including electronic, mechanical, photocopying,
recording or otherwise, without the prior written consent
of the author and publisher.

The Slug, the Snail and their Tale

With Idioms

Sara Dufton

Illustrations by Freddie Btesh

STELLAR BOOKS

Sidney was in a rut. He was bored and fed up with the slow pace of his life at the bottom of the garden; this was not how he had planned on spending the summer.

He was, literally, in a rut!

He had fallen down the side of a tyre track, which had been left by the gardener's small tractor yesterday evening. It took so much energy for the small slug to pull himself out of such a depression but, he thought, here goes, it's now or never.

Sidney had dreamt many times about the different ways he could escape this slug-eat-slug world and become an independent, young slug fending for himself. Here was his big chance. He slid over to what appeared to be a large piece of wood sticking up out of the soil, but was actually one of the gardener's spades. Having spent pretty much all of his life living under the dark, damp soil, Sidney was nervous but excited as he shuffled over and began his ascent.

His slippery, slimy mucous provided the lubrication he needed to push himself along. As he got higher and higher the wind seemed to be blowing harder and harder and he became frightened and felt very much like a fish out of water. Sidney knew about the dangers of the wind and the sun, having seen lots of other slugs dry up as a result of too much exposure, but at last he was at the top.

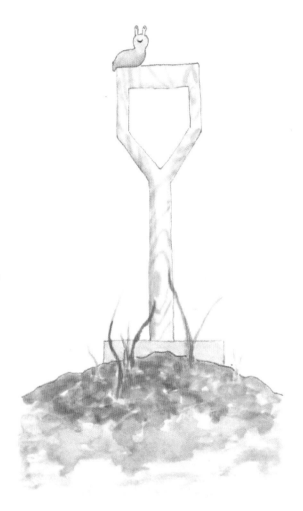

Exhausted and hungry, yet exhilarated, he felt very proud of his endeavours. While he was usually small fry in his slug community, he now felt very important, as he could see the whole world from up here. Now, he thought, was his opportunity to leave the fold and have an adventure.

Just next to the spade was the neighbour's fence and directly alongside was an old oak tree. Sidney decided to crawl along the fence and up into the tree by means of a wooden ladder that had been built by the children next door to get into their tree house.

At last, Sidney found himself in the tree house. He was exhausted. He helped himself to a supper of mould and lichen from the damp, wooden floor and bedded down in a cosy corner on a wet pile of leaves.

The next morning he awoke with a start when he realised he wasn't alone. Sasha the snail was already breakfasting in another corner of the tree house.

"Morning," said Sidney, feeling a little nervous. He much preferred his own company and was not used to mixing with other molluscs. Sasha replied:

"*Bonjour, je m'appelle Sasha. Comment allez-vous?*"
Sidney did not immediately grasp what Sasha had said and he hesitated. Sasha continued in her native French with a little bit of English thrown in.

"*Je suis perdu!* Oh how do you say this *en Anglais?* I think I am lost."

"Oh dear," said Sidney. "Where are you trying to get to?"

"I am trying to get *chez moi en France* to a town called Calais, which I think is over the other side of the sea. I do not know how I came to be *en Angleterre*. I had been enjoying a day at the seaside along with many other people. The next thing I knew, it all went very dark for a few hours and then I fell onto the floor and landed in the children's sandpit at the bottom of this garden.*"*

Sidney realised this was his big chance to escape to a new world and promptly offered to help Sasha return home to France. This was to be the start of their journey together.

Sidney, who was not wet behind the ears, had realised exactly what had happened to poor Sasha.

As soon as she had mentioned landing in the sandpit, he struck gold – well, only figuratively. She had been brought home from the beach in the boot of the family's car, probably either inside or stuck to the bottom of one of the children's buckets. She had then been discarded into the sandpit when they arrived home.

"Yes!" he exclaimed. This was to be his golden opportunity to get out of his slow and sluggish life. Sidney shimmied over to where Sasha was finishing her breakfast.

"I think I have realised how you got here, so now all we need to do is get back into a bucket and wait to be transported back to the seaside. That is, if you don't mind me coming with you?" proclaimed Sidney, deciding that he needed to be assertive. He was equally worried that he might be making an ass of himself.

Sasha turned around and moved rather more quickly than her usual snail's pace and, indeed, looked remarkably like she now had a bad case of ants in her pants! She was clearly very excited at the possibility of heading home with Sidney as her companion.

It was time to start making plans.

The sun had been shining all day, so to avoid the potential hazard of drying out and losing their slime – and their ability to move – they decided to wait until dusk. As soon as it got dark, they set off on the steep, slow descent of the tree trunk. Sasha, with no head for heights and with a lot of butterflies in her tummy, followed Sidney who appeared to be gliding quite easily. Sasha shimmied along behind him using his slime for added acceleration.

Once at the bottom, the two new buddies wandered along through the very overgrown garden, stopping to munch on the occasional leaf. After what seemed like an incredibly long time, the grass became patchy and the ground felt very gritty under their smooth, soggy bodies. Sasha had a serious case of *déjà vu,* she had been here before. They had arrived at the children's sandpit. Sidney had guessed right. This is definitely how she got here.

"*Je t'adores Sidney, tu es très intelligent!*" exclaimed Sasha.

Rather thrilled by this compliment – well, he assumed it was a compliment, judging by the way Sasha was beaming at him – Sidney felt like the bee's knees. He peered down into the large sandpit and noticed to his dismay that buried in the sand were a number of spades of all shapes and sizes, a couple of buckets, some colourful plastic forks, a tennis ball and even a pair of sandals. Now he had a dilemma. A bucket could be their mode of transport but how did they know which bucket and spade the children were going to pick out? This was a real fly in the ointment.

Once in the sandpit, Sidney inspected the buckets more closely and noticed that one of them had a large split in the bottom. He thought it would make more sense to use the other one. It was shaped like a fabulous castle which he was sure the children would prefer.

Sidney and Sasha snuggled down inside the base of the bucket, starting to feel as snug as two bugs in a rug, but then Sidney had an awful thought. He turned to Sasha and said,

"What if the children didn't like slugs and snails and emptied them out of the bucket before taking it to the car?"

"Zut alors!" cried Sasha. What were they going to do?

This had opened a whole new can of worms. Sidney was becoming dizzy, gliding around the sandpit trying desperately to find the answer. Out of the corner of his eye he noticed a large, bright, red spade, larger than all of the others in the sandpit. If he could move that spade into their bucket, he was certain the children would not notice him and Sasha hiding behind it, as long as they disguised themselves in some sand.

· · ·

Just at that moment, a large black cat appeared at the edge of the sandpit. Sidney had seen this cat before, usually being sent on a wild goose chase by a rather annoying small brown dog. Woody the terrier caused absolute mayhem whenever he was in the garden. No sooner had Sidney thought about this than the pesky dog ran down the garden straight towards the very worried-looking cat.

The cat immediately scarpered across the sand, scattering all the brightly coloured buckets and spades across the sandpit, miraculously shifting the large, bright, red spade right next to the bucket that the two friendly molluscs were resting in.

"*Ooh la la!*" exclaimed Sasha, who had woken with a start. "*Qu'est-ce qui se passe? Je suis très...* how do you say *en Anglais...* frightened?"

Sidney certainly did not hold back and gave Sasha a comforting hug, feeling and looking rather like the cat that had got the cream.

He couldn't have planned the escape any better if he had tried. The dog and cat had certainly worked their magic, even though they were somewhat unaware of the situation.

The sky was lovely and blue with no sign of rain. It was not ideal weather for slugs and snails but it was a great day for children to visit the beach.

Just at that moment, the children came running down the garden and began gathering up various items from the sandpit. Sidney held on to Sasha tightly to try and stop them both from falling out of the bucket if it happened to be selected. He also liked the idea of being close to her and figured he was killing two birds with one stone.

"Goodness gracious me!" muttered Sidney to himself as he realised their colourful bucket had, indeed, been selected from the gritty sandpit and was now being carried aloft to a safer haven.